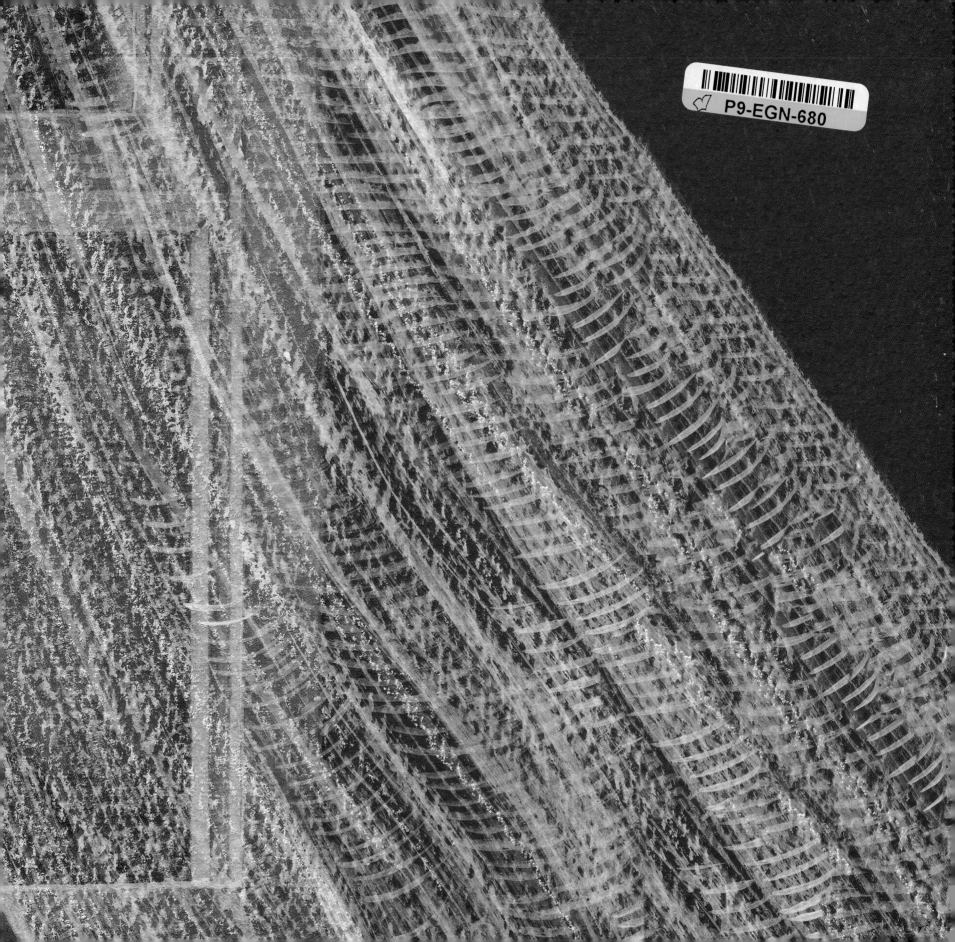

The World CHAMPION

Text copyright © 2011 by Sean Taylor
Illustrations copyright © 2011 by Jimmy Liao

First U.S. edition 2011

Library of Congress Cataloging-in-Publication Data
Taylor, Sean, date.
The world champion of staying awake / Sean Taylor ; [illustrations by] Jimmy Liao. —1st U.S. ed.
p.   cm.
Summary: At bedtime, Stella must find a way to make her toys fall asleep before she can sleep.
ISBN 978-0-7636-4957-9
[1. Bedtime—Fiction. 2. Toys—Fiction.]   I. Jimi, ill. II. Title.
PZ7.T21783Wo 2010
[E]—dc22   2009051511

CCP 16 15 14 13 12 11
10 9 8 7 6 5 4 3 2

Printed in Shenzhen, Guangdong, China

This book was typeset in Memphis. The illustrations were done in watercolor.

Candlewick Press
99 Dover Street
Somerville, Massachusetts 02144

visit us at www.candlewick.com

# of Staying Awake

SEAN TAYLOR

illustrated by JIMMY LIAO

CANDLEWICK PRESS

For Christine
S. T.

For Roro
J. L.

"Good night, Stella," says Dad.
"Time to go to bed."

But how can Stella go to bed?
She still has Cherry Pig,
Thunderbolt the puppet mouse,
and Beanbag Frog to get to sleep.

"I'm a bit wide awake,"
snuffles Cherry Pig.

"I'm a *lot* wide awake!"
calls out Thunderbolt.

And Beanbag Frog is worse than
wide awake. He's going hoppety-hop.

"Stoppety-stop!" says Stella.
"It's time to go to bed."

"I'm not going to sleep!"
calls out Thunderbolt.

"Sleep is too slow!"
croaks Beanbag Frog.

**"I'm the world champion of
staying awake!"** says Cherry Pig.

But Stella is good at thinking
up ways to get them to sleep.

So she puts them on her pillow.
"Can you dream the pillow into
something?" asks Cherry Pig.

"Yes," says Stella.

"It's a ship."

And it is.

The pillow ship rocks.
The pillow ship sways.
The pillow ship sails
across the waves.

In the deep water
under the boat,
jellyfish, sharks, and
sea horses float.

But down in the cabin,
you'll come to no harm.
You'll be warm as a cat
sleeping inside a barn.

So snuggle your feet,
    snuggle your knees,
    and let yourself sway
    over the seas.

Quietly, Stella checks.

Cherry Pig is asleep.

But Beanbag Frog asks,
"Is jelly made from jellyfish?"

And Thunderbolt is calling out,
"The world champion of staying awake is actually ME!"

"How am I ever going to
get you two to sleep?"
Stella says with a sigh.

"With presents, toys, fireworks,
and spicy-sausage pizza?"
suggests Thunderbolt.

"It's not time for anything like that," Stella tells them. "It's time to *shut your eyes*."

"I've shut my eyes, but my feet are completely woken up," says Beanbag Frog in a very bouncy voice.

So Stella puts them
in her shoe box.

"Can you dream this box into
something?" asks Thunderbolt.

"Yes," says Stella.

"It's a train."

And it is.

Outside, the air
  is cold with rain,
but it's warm and dry
  on the midnight train.

The silver wheels
  spin around on the track,
on their way over
  the mountains and back.

And as it chugs
  and clatters and steams,
the train will carry you
  into your dreams . . .

dreams of long journeys
and dinosaur eggs,
dreams of white horses
with galloping legs.

"Who's the world champion
  of staying awake now?"
whispers Stella.

Thunderbolt lifts his head and says,
**"I'm the world champion of . . .
  going to sleep."**

Then he closes his eyes.

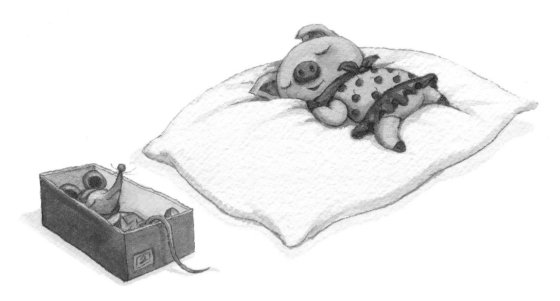

So that leaves Beanbag Frog.   Is he asleep?

No. He's not.
He's going
hoppety-hop
again.

"How many years is
it to my birthday?"
he asks Stella.

"I can't believe you're still
awake!" she whispers.

"I can!" says his croaky voice.
**"The world champion of staying
awake must actually be ME!"**

"Yes," says Stella.

So Stella puts him in the toy basket.
"Can you dream our basket into
something?" asks Beanbag Frog.

And it is.

"It's a balloon."

The starship balloon
flies off and away,
leaving behind
the last of today.

Through air as quiet
as fallen snow,
up and up and up
you go . . .

up so high that it's best
 to stop
if you feel like going
 hoppety-hop.

And what's around you
 as you rise?
The sparkling necklaces
 of the skies.

Stella checks. Beanbag Frog is lying with his head on one arm.

Not a croak. Not a bounce. Not a hoppety-hop.

"They're *all* fast asleep," she whispers.

And she tucks them, one by one, into bed.

So the world champion of staying awake
must actually be Stella.

Or maybe not.